Who made thos

An Ivy and Ma

Written by Juliet Clare Bell
Illustrated by Gustavo Mazali
with Szépvölgyi Eszter

Collins

What's in this story?

Listen and say 1

snow

winter
snowman
snow child
snow dog

It was a Monday afternoon in the winter holidays. There was snow on the ground. There was snow on Ivy and Mack's new jackets and gloves.

"Are you coming?" said Grandpa. "Banjo needs his walk."

“Wow!” said Mack. “Look at all the snow!”

“Let’s make a snowman,” said Ivy.

They made a big body and a head. They gave the snowman eyes, a mouth and some arms.

"Good work," said Grandpa.

"Hmmm ..." said Mack.

They walked home for lunch.

“Can we come back?” asked Ivy.

Grandpa smiled. “Yes! Banjo and I love walking in the winter!”

“Good,” said Mack. “We can bring a scarf and a carrot for the snowman!”

On Tuesday afternoon, Ivy, Mack, Grandpa and Banjo went back to their snowman.

Now there were two snowmen.
“Look, there are two snowmen. And they both have noses!” said Ivy.

“And they both have scarves, too!” said Mack.

They finished their snowman and made a snow child. Grandpa gave the snow child some arms, too.

"Look! They're holding hands!" said Mack.

"See you soon, snow family!" said Ivy.

On Wednesday afternoon, there were two snow children!

"Look, another snow child!" said Mack. "And look at their scarves!"

"I've got an idea," said Ivy. "Let's come back in the morning and see!"

On Thursday morning, Mum and Dad came to look. There were no people, but next to the snowmen and the snow children there was a new friend!

"Look, a snow dog!" said Mack and Ivy.

Mum and Dad started to build a snow house.

Ivy wrote a message.

"Hello! We love the snow family! The snow dog is great! Please meet us here on Friday morning. Bring food and hot drinks!"

It was Friday morning. Dad made some hot chocolate. Ivy and Mack got some biscuits.

“Right, let’s go and get Grandpa!” said Mum.

Mack opened the door. “Oh, no! Where is all the snow?” he said.

“Do you think the snow family are OK?” he asked Ivy.

"I don't want the snowmen to fall down!" said Mack.

"They're fine," said Ivy. "But look at these new snow dogs. They're *Banjo* snow dogs!"

Ivy saw a boy and his dad. She waved.
“I think *THEY* made them!” she said.

The boy's name was Sam. "I made this snowman. And this snow child and the big dog," he said.

"What about *those*?" said Mack. He pointed at the Banjo snow dogs.

"Hello!" It was Ivy's friend Mina.

"Are these *your* snow dogs?" asked Mack.

"Yes! I made them!" said Mina.

The hot chocolate was nice and hot. Mina and Sam looked up. "It's snowing again!"

Ivy picked up some snow. "What are you thinking, Ivy?" asked Mack.

"These snowmen are very clever!" said Ivy. "They can throw snowballs."

"Quick, Ivy. Let's throw them back! This is the best snowball game," said Mack.

And it was.

Picture dictionary

Listen and repeat 

1 Look and order the story

2 Listen and say  

Collins

Published by Collins
An imprint of HarperCollins*Publishers*
Westerhill Road
Bishopbriggs
Glasgow
G64 2QT

HarperCollins*Publishers*
1st Floor, Watermarque Building
Ringsend Road
Dublin 4
Ireland

William Collins' dream of knowledge for all began with the publication of his first book in 1819.

A self-educated mill worker, he not only enriched millions of lives, but also founded a flourishing publishing house. Today, staying true to this spirit, Collins books are packed with inspiration, innovation and practical expertise. They place you at the centre of a world of possibility and give you exactly what you need to explore it.

10 9 8 7 6 5 4 3 2

ISBN 978-0-00-839655-8

www.collins.co.uk/elt

British Library Cataloguing in Publication Data

A catalogue record for this publication is available from the British Library.

Author: Juliet Clare Bell
Lead illustrator: Gustavo Mazali (Beehive)
Copy illustrator: Szépvölgyi Eszter (Beehive)
Series editor: Rebecca Adlard
Commissioning editor: Zoë Clarke
Publishing manager: Lisa Todd
Product managers: Jennifer Hall and Caroline Green
In-house editor: Alma Puts Keren
Project manager: Emily Hooton
Editor: Deborah Friedland
Proofreaders: Natalie Murray and Michael Lamb
Cover designer: Kevin Robbins
Typesetter: 2Hoots Publishing Services Ltd
Audio produced by id audio, London
Reading guide author: Julie Penn
Production controller: Rachel Weaver
Printed and bound by: GPS Group, Slovenia

MIX
Paper from responsible sources
FSC™ C007454

This book is produced from independently certified FSC™ paper to ensure responsible forest management.

For more information visit: **www.harpercollins.co.uk/green**

Download the audio for this book and a reading guide for parents and teachers at www.collins.co.uk/839655